CONTINUATION - A CONSOLATION DUET SPECIAL EDITION

CORINNE MICHAELS

Continuation

A Consolation Duet Compliation

By: Corinne Michaels

COCKBLOCKED

CHAPTER ONE

"You're going to behave, Liam. I don't care what you say, this is a big deal for any girl, and I swear to God that you will be on the couch if you screw this up for her." I point at him, but all he does is grumble.

"How are you so okay with this?"

"I'm not okay with this," I sigh and touch the side of his face. "I just have to be a grown up, like you will be."

He shakes his head. "This isn't fun."

"Nope, it definitely blows, but it's prom and part of the ritual."

It isn't easy watching my beautiful little girl grow up. I want to freeze time, make her stay the sweet child who said funny words forever. Time doesn't work that way, though.

Aarabelle is seventeen years old.

She's practically a woman.

"Prom is when kids have sex, Lee."

Here we go again. "I didn't have sex at prom," I inform him.

"Well, neither is Aarabelle, so at least we'll be two for two."

I'm not even going to ask how he plans to stop her if that's what she wants to do because that's a rabbit hole I'll never get out of.

"What's the plan, Athair?" Shane, our son, asks Liam as he walks in the living room.

Our kids both call him that because there was never a day that he wanted to be just "Liam" to Aara. Since his Irish roots are very deep, we use the Gaelic word for father. Liam never wanted to take Aaron's place as her father, but he *is* that in every sense of the word. He's here when it's hard. He cares for her when she's sick, helps with homework, and is her father. He's the constant in her life, and her relationship with him shows that.

Shane decided it was cool so he uses it too.

Boys.

These two are ridiculous. Absolutely out of their minds. Shane is fourteen, but almost two inches taller than his sister. He has dark brown hair and blue eyes like his father. The only thing he got from me is his IQ. Shane is a ladies man through and through. I can't think about you how many girls call his cell phone because if I did, it would make me want to scream and lock him inside a cage.

Liam had a long talk with him about girls, which I'm sure included a bunch of that's-my-boy type crap, but when it comes to Aara? Forget it.

That girl is lucky he doesn't have her stashed in an ivory tower somewhere.

"The plan is we teach the jackoff coming to take my daughter to prom how we roll around here."

"And how do we roll, babe?" I ask.

"SEAL style."

"Oh, Jesus," I mutter under my breath and leave the room.

I head upstairs, looking at the photos that line the wall. Time goes by so fast. I feel as though it was just yesterday that Liam and I fell in love. I remember how he made me smile when all I wanted was to cry, how he cared for me when I was enduring the loss of Aaron, and just how precious our love is.

I see the photo of Aarabelle from when she was just about two years old. In it, she's sitting on Liam's shoulders as they chase the geese at the park. Our wedding picture, taken at a moment when not even God himself could have convinced me that one day I would love him more. A picture from the day we brought Shane home from the hospital.

It's all there in little permanent memories.

Now we have teenagers who make me question my life choices.

"Mom," Aara calls from the bathroom.

"I'm here." I push through the door, and she turns to smile at me.

"Can you help me with this dress? I can't get the zipper up."

Aarabelle is truly beautiful. And I don't just think that because I'm her mother. She really is naturally gorgeous.

I'm sure the years of dance have helped with her figure, but the girl doesn't wear makeup and is still stunning. She got my blonde hair and Aaron's eyes. She's a perfect mix of her parents.

I slide the zipper up for her and then adjust the skirt. I don't know when dresses started to become two pieces, but she was adamant this is what she was wearing.

"All done," I say as I touch her shoulder. "You look gorgeous."

She smiles in the mirror. "I wish Dad could be here."

"I know."

There isn't much to say to comfort her. Sometimes things just don't work the way we want them to, and when it comes to Aaron, no truer words apply. Life is ever-changing, and she learned that at an early age.

"Did you talk to Athair?" she asks. "About being nice to Chase and not totally embarrassing me?"

Oh, I talked to him all right, but it didn't go the way she would've liked. He went on and on about punk teenagers and how it's his job and right as a father to scare them from his daughter.

"I did, but Aara, you know how he is . . ."

She sighs. "Yeah, protective and crazy."

"Pretty much."

"Can't you . . . I don't know . . . threaten to beat him or something?"

"I did, but he's not exactly known for listening to me."

Aarabelle groans. "Well, maybe he'll at least try not to embarrass me."

That's funny. There's not a chance in hell he's going to do that, but we can at least hope he doesn't scare her date off. "I wouldn't count on it, honey. This is the first time you're bringing your boyfriend around, I would expect loads of hell."

"I can't bring boys around here because I have my idiot brother and Athair!"

I wish I could completely sympathize with her, but it isn't something I'm complaining about either.

Now for the awkward conversation that must happen.

"Aara, can you sit?"

"Sure," she draws out.

"Listen, it's prom night, and I know that sometimes you get a little rowdy." I pause when her face scrunches.

Believe me, kid, I don't want to talk about this either.

"Mom," Aara puts her hand up, "if you're talking about sex, gross and no way because Chase is just a *friend*, for the millionth time. If you're worried about drinking, don't be. I'm not stupid."

"No, but you're a teenager."

She's a good girl by all counts. Aarabelle is honor roll, top in her class, and a very accomplished dancer.

Her life is ballet and nothing will stop her.

"I'm not having sex, Mom!"

"You damn well better not be," Liam bellows from behind me, making her cringe.

"Well, I'm not. He's a friend—again, not my boyfriend. You guys are so weird!"

"Whatever, Chase William Leighton has a clean driving

record, is currently on the honor roll, and lives in Baylake Pines —I have his exact address here in case you're home late." Liam hold up a sheet of paper for emphasis. "His parents are Katy and Josh, and he has a younger sister."

"Oh, my God!" Aarabelle yells. "Are you insane? You had him investigated?"

She has no idea the lengths this man will go to ensure her safety. Liam gives me a look because he's taking the heat for this one. He wasn't the one who had Chase's information checked, it was me.

I trust Aarabelle, but working for a security company has its perks sometimes.

"Of course we did," he says unapologetically.

"I can't believe this."

"Believe it, princess. A father will do just about anything for his kids." Liam steps into the room and looks at her dress. "Where's the rest of it?" he asks, waving his hand up and down.

"At the store." The sarcasm is thick as she rolls her eyes at him.

"Funny, go back and get one that's not missing material."

"Dear God," I mutter to the ceiling.

"It's fine, Athair. It's a dress. All the girls have them just like this."

Liam rubs the bridge of his nose. "You look beautiful, princess. Truly. You also aren't leaving in that."

"Mom!" Aarabelle spins to face me as if expecting me to stick up for her. I told her he wouldn't approve of it, but she wouldn't budge.

Having kids is so much fun.

"Don't cry to her, I'm not letting you out of the house in half a dress. Your stomach is showing, Aarabelle!"

Hadn't I told her he would say that?

Yes. Yes I did.

Overprotective and Liam should be synonymous. She's his little girl that still climbs on his back, runs into his arms when he gets home from work, and wants him to teach her how to shoot.

He doesn't get that none of that is reality anymore.

"I'm not changing. This is more than my bikini I wear on the beach." Her lip trembles.

I see the tears threaten to form and step in. "You've helped raise her into a beautiful girl, you have to let her shine. She's wearing the dress, put your macho crap away and knock it off."

"She can shine wearing a sea bag."

"Liam." I sigh.

"Natalie."

I turn to Aarabelle. "Finish getting ready, and we'll meet you downstairs. You don't worry about him." Then I shove my husband out the door. When we're far enough away that I know she won't hear me, I shove his chest. "Really?"

"What?"

"Are you nuts?"

He raises his brow. "Only about you."

"Don't be cute, Liam."

"I can't help it."

He makes it so hard to stay mad at him. "She spent hours searching for the perfect dress. She needs you not to be a lunatic father for once and be the man I know you are."

Liam smirks and taps my nose. "You're giving me more credit than I deserve. I am a lunatic father, and that boy is going to shit himself when he comes here. Accept that, and we'll be much happier."

I really pray Aarabelle doesn't put Exlax in his brownies next time she bakes, but if she does, I won't blame her.

"What am I going to do with you?" I ask rhetorically.

"I can think of a few things . . ."

"I bet you can." I giggle as my hands glide up his strong arms.

"If I behave, will you be naughty later tonight?"

I'm bartering him sex for not acting like a dumbass. The

things we do for our kids. Who am I kidding? This really only benefits me.

"I guess you'll have to see."

"Don't tease me, woman."

I sigh and press my lips to his. "I thought you liked a little teasing."

Liam pushes our bodies back so he has complete control. I feel him harden as he moves so he's at that perfect spot. "I think it's you that likes to be teased."

"Gross," Shane says as he gets to the top of the stairs. "Seriously, you guys are ridiculous."

Liam shrugs. "Cover your eyes then."

Shane shakes his head. "I need bleach and some kind of memory eraser."

"That can be arranged," Liam tosses back as I try to shove him away. "Where are you going?"

"Downstairs." I try to move, but it's pointless. He has me right where he wants me, and he's ten times stronger than I am.

The doorbell rings, and he groans. "I really have to be nice to this tool?"

"For Aara."

"Fine."

We trudge down the stairs with Liam grumbling about locking her in her room until she's thirty. When I open the door, I'm a little shocked to find that it isn't her date.

"Douchecanoe!" Mark yells as he steps inside. "I brought reinforcements."

Sure enough, in walks Jackson, Quinn, and Ben—the new guy. Ben is heading up the protection detail side of the company, and he might be the only person in the company who scares me a little. The guy is huge, and I don't know that he knows how to smile, except when he looks at Gretchen . . .

Which is definitely the reason that Liam had him come.

"What the hell are you clowns doing here?" I ask. "No one told you to be here."

"Liam invited us," Mark informs me.

"Well, this is me telling you to leave." I hold the door open and point outside.

There is no way this is going to go over well. If Aarabelle sees that her uncles came to join the party, she might lose it.

Mark laughs. "Not this time, Sparkles."

"Jackson?" I plead since he's the most reasonable of this lot.

"I have girls, this is par for the course," he says with a shrug. "I expect the same courtesy. This is what we do."

"Your funeral," I say. "Aara is not going to like this."

Jackson grins. "That's the point. We know what boys think, we were those boys, we want to hunt those boys down and beat them if they have those thoughts about our girls."

As if they didn't break hearts as adults. Please. I've had ringside seats to their circus for most of my life.

Right on cue, Aarabelle comes down the stairs. The look of horror on her face is almost comical. "No, no, no, no way! No! You have half the SEAL team here?"

"I protect my family," Liam explains as he pops the top off his beer.

"No one in the world has this much insanity in their family!" Aara screeches.

"I swear," I warn them all in a harsh whisper, "that if you ruin this day for my daughter, I will make each one of you pay for it . . . got me?"

They may be big bad former SEALs, but I'm not afraid of any of them. Plus, their wives will ensure it continues far past the rain I bring.

"We're just going to scare him a little," Quinn says. "This is the fun part of what we do."

"If she sheds one tear"—I point around the room—"dead."

"Isn't she cute when she gets all mama bear?" Liam says and I level him with a stare.

"You really shouldn't test me."

"Sweetheart, that's all I live for." He smirks and leans back.

There's no point in continuing the conversation. I know that he knows better than to really try his hand about this.

Satisfied that they won't do anything stupid, I head in the kitchen as the group of guys talk about sports and deployments. Aara comes in, typing on her phone.

"I'm going to meet him there," she says.

"Aara."

"No way am I going to let him show up here with them in the living room. Uncle Mark is going to . . . I don't even want to think about it."

"Your family just loves you. They protect what they care about." I try to explain their craziness.

"Yeah, well, they're nuts."

"Yeah, they are."

I push her phone down from her face and tilt her chin up. "I'm proud of you."

"Thanks, Mom."

"And you look beautiful."

She smiles. "I look like you did when you went to prom with Dad."

God that feels like forever ago, well, it was. I wore a deep plum-colored dress with my hair down, and Aarabelle is doing the same.

"Well, you look much prettier than I did."

"Your date is here!" One of the guys yells from the living room.

"Please help me," she gives me one last plea.

Oh, honey, if only I could.

We exit the kitchen, and I swear that I don't even know what alternate universe I just stepped into.

How long were we in there?

Clearly long enough for the guys to change into full gear and paint their faces as if they were on some mission in Afghanistan instead of shooting the shit in my living room.

"Liam Dempsey!" I yell as he hoists his gun over his shoulder. "Are you on drugs?"

"It's not loaded."

"Not the point!"

"I'm just introducing the kid to what it's going to be like to date my daughter." He grins through the face paint, and I could get lost in those blue eyes I'd know anywhere.

Then I remember I'm pissed at him.

"Come on in, son," Jackson's voice is booming as he pulls the boy inside.

Aarabelle marches through them, pushing their chests so she can get there. "Don't listen to any of them, Chase. They're all . . . dead to me."

The kid looks like he could shit himself. I sort of feel bad for him.

Shane comes running down the stairs to watch the shit show. "Hey, Chase." He grins. "Remember what we talked about . . . this isn't even half of it."

"You're so stupid." Aarabelle sneers at her brother. "Go away."

"You can say that to me, but what about Athair?"

Her face pales as Liam walks over, wipes his brow with his sleeve, smearing the paint. "So, you like my daughter?"

"Ye-yes, sir," Chase stutters.

"Do you think you're good enough to go out with her?" Mark steps in.

He looks over at the tallest of the men crowding my living room. "Yes, sir."

"So you think you're better than Aara?" Liam takes a step closer.

"No, no, sir. I just mean . . ."

Jackson clears his throat. "He just means that Aarabelle is good, but not as good as he is."

"I didn't say that," Chase tries to clarify.

"So, wait, you're good enough for her, but she isn't better

than you?" Quinn asks as he slips a knife out of its sheath and acts as if he's cleaning his nail.

"I think Aarabelle is great," Chase tries.

"But not amazing?" Liam asks.

There are no right answers here. No matter what he says, they'll twist it.

"Mom!" Aara looks at me for help.

I'm always the one trying to keep these idiots out of trouble, but the mother in me is also enjoying this boy being aware that there are four very skilled men ready to protect her. It leads me to believe he will be on his best behavior.

"Chase," I smile warmly, "why don't we head outside for some pictures?"

She practically throws him out the door just to get away from the firing squad. When I get to the door, I turn and face them. "You guys are bad, but that was funny."

Liam steps forward, takes my face in his hands, and presses his lips to mine. "I'm having fun with this."

I roll my eyes. "It shows."

He kisses me again, surely getting green and black on my face.

"All right, let's line up for a photo!" Jackson says as I stand in the doorway laughing.

———

"YOU CAN'T SAY it's not a good photo," Liam says as he leans against the doorframe with nothing but a towel on.

"It's ridiculous, but it's a good one."

Aarabelle endured another twenty minutes of her father and uncles giving her hell before she was finally able to get into the limo.

She sent both Liam and me a text with a photo from her phone.

It has her on one end, Chase on the other, and the idiots in the middle. It's really comical, but it's also a sad reality of her dating life. She'll always have these dopes in the middle of it if they have a say.

I put the phone on the table beside me and climb up onto my knees. "You know . . . I thought it was really sexy seeing you in your gear again."

He smirks and steps toward the bed. "How sexy?"

"On a scale of one to ten?" I bite my bottom lip and pretend to ponder. "An eight."

"Just an eight?" Liam asks as he reaches the bed.

"I think I know what would bring it to a ten . . ." I lean closer, pull his towel free, and then toss it across the bed. "That for starters."

"I like the way you think," he says and grabs my hips.

Liam tosses me down onto the bed and pulls my shorts off. "Am I getting warmer?"

I love when he's this way. His confidence that borders on cocky makes me thankful that he's mine—all mine.

"Definitely."

He kisses my stomach before moving lower. "Now?"

"Liam." I hiss his name when his tongue swipes across my clit.

"Am I at a ten now, sweetheart?"

I moan, unable to form words.

"Or are we at a nine?"

Why is he talking? "Don't stop," I beg.

"Yes, ma'am." He chuckles and then gets back to work.

My hands grip the pillow, pulling it over my face so when I scream I don't wake the neighbors. He circles my clit, making my legs shake as I climb higher. I'm hovering on the edge, sitting in that place where it's almost painful because I need to release. Liam knows exactly what he's doing, and I'm not complaining one bit.

I start to twist when it becomes too much, but his strong hands hold my legs down. He moves his tongue in lazy circles, keeping me on the edge, and it's as though I'm being ripped apart.

"Liam!" The muffled sound of my voice is desperate. "Please!"

"Take the pillow off your face, I want to hear every fucking noise tonight."

Aarabelle is at the after prom, and Shane is at a sleepover. For once, we don't have to worry about kids hearing us.

I do as he says and toss the pillow onto the floor. "Yes," I whimper as he circles my clit. "God, Liam!"

My head thrashes from side to side as pleasure overtakes me. I writhe beneath him, my pulse races, and I bite down on my lip.

I'm hanging on the edge, ready to go over, needing to release the pressure. Liam continues his slow assault, taking his time to bring me to the brink. "Yes. There. Oh. Jesus!" My fingers grip his hair as he sucks hard while flicking my clit, and I explode.

My orgasm rages on and on as he continues to pull every ounce of pleasure from my body.

Once he's satisfied, he climbs up so we're face to face.

My eyes open, and a blissed out smile tugs at my lips. He's perfect, and he's one of those men who look better the older he gets. I touch his strong jawline, which is covered in a beard long enough for me to run my fingers through it. His crystal blue eyes are filled with so much love that it takes my breath away.

I'm a very lucky woman.

"Why are you smiling?" he asks.

"Because you're mine."

He moves my hair off my face and smiles back. "Damn fucking right you are. Now, I'm going to make love to my wife and make her scream my name a few more times."

I move my fingers through his hair. "She would really like that."

Liam shifts as I part my legs, giving him the in that we are both craving.

He pushes forward, taking me, owning me, loving me the way that only he can.

Our eyes stay trained on one another. "You feel so good," he says before kissing me.

"You always feel good."

"I love you so much, sweetheart. So much."

"I love you more."

He starts to rock back and forth, giving me all the love in the world. When we're together, life makes sense. We've been lucky that he hasn't deployed in the last two years.

Liam is the other half to my soul, and being a SEAL's wife means I have to share him . . . and possibly lose him.

I never want to live in a world without him, and my eyes fill with tears before I can push the thoughts away.

He's here. He's alive and came home to me, just like he promised he'd do.

"Am I hurting you?" he asks quickly.

I shake my head and wipe the tears from my cheek. "No, baby, I'm just allowing myself to feel how much I love you."

"Fuck, Natalie." Liam groans as he moves faster, pushing so deep inside me that we're completely one.

I need more. I need all of him.

His fingers tangle in my hair, and he squeezes as he roars.

We lay like this for a few moments, breathing each other in, reveling in the moment.

He doesn't move for so long that I start to think that he fell asleep—inside me. I wait another minute, and he finally turns his head toward me.

"Hi." I smile.

"Hi."

I run my fingers up and down his spine. "You all right?"

"Oh, I'm very all right."

I shake my head at the playful tone. "Are you planning on getting up?"

He grunts. "I'm fine."

"Liam." I giggle as he tucks his face against the crook of my neck.

"What? It makes it easier for round two."

He's a mess. A beautiful mess. "Come on, babe. I need to get up."

Liam hoists himself up a little, his smile is lazy and beyond sexy. Everything about him makes me happy. He runs his thumb against my lips, touching each part of my face. "Each day I ask myself what in the world I did to deserve you."

"You were you," I reply as if it's the only answer in the world.

"And you were meant to be mine."

He presses his lips to mine, and once again, tears spring to my eyes. "Then I guess it's a pretty good thing we found each other, huh?"

Liam nods. "You've given me everything a man could ever want in his life."

My heart swells, and I brush my thumb across his cheek. "Yeah?"

"I have a son and a daughter who I would lie down my life for. A woman who loves me more than I deserve. You're the other half to my soul, Lee. You think I say this shit because I'm so sweet or whatever crap you tell Catherine and Charlie, but the truth is that I wouldn't be who I am without you."

"Why do you have to be so amazing all the time?"

Liam rolls off to the side, pulling me against his chest. "Because I love you, sweetheart. I know you're tough and you don't need anyone to take care of you, but I see the cracks."

My head sits on my hand while I look at the man I love with my whole heart. "You keep coming home to me, and I'll keep spackling."

"You're not the handiest person."

I laugh and slap his chest. "You shouldn't talk, Mr. Duct Tape, you're the one who taped your daughter's diaper and then tied the Christmas tree to the ceiling."

He shrugs. "You love me."

"That I do, I most definitely do."

"I love you. You know what else I love?" Liam asks.

There's mischief in his eyes, and I can only imagine what the hell is coming next. "Now I'm scared."

Liam pushes my hair out of my eyes with a wicked grin. "Chocolate."

"Oh, I can get with some chocolate!"

We climb out of bed and throw on some clothes. Once in the kitchen, I grab the bag of KitKats I keep hidden from Aarabelle and Shane.

"That's where you keep the stash?" He laughs as I'm climbing down from the chair I used to get in the top cabinet.

"Don't judge. I need my candy when you're gone."

"Come here," Liam says, holding a hand out to me. "I want to show you something."

"Okay," I say hesitantly.

Liam pulls me out of the kitchen, grabs the blanket off the back of the couch, and tugs me back toward the hallway.

"What are you doing?"

"Showing you what it's going to be like when the kids are out of the house. Sex in all the rooms. Starting with the dining room."

CHAPTER TWO

"Where is she?" Liam asks as he paces the hall as he pulls the beanie off his head.

"Calm down!"

"Don't tell me to calm down, that little cocksucker was supposed to have her home five minutes ago," he bellows.

Sometimes he's this calm, level-headed man that I love being around. Then, we have this madman who makes me crazy by being a complete freak show.

"Liam, sit down."

He goes to the window, pushes the blinds down, slips his beanie back on, and then grumbles again. "I can't. This little shit is probably—"

"Is, nothing," I finish. "They went to a movie across town, you and I know better than anything that traffic here is horrible."

My phone vibrates.

AARABELLE: There's an accident on Shore Drive. I'm trying. Please tell Athair we're coming and not to shoot anything or anyone.

Me: Okay. Just get here safely.

"See?" I hold my phone up. "She's on her way, but there's an accident."

He laughs. "Yeah, right. She was probably doing God knows what and lost track of time."

"Oh, so she acted like you as a teenager?"

Liam levels me with a stare. "Don't try to send me over the edge."

I'm pretty sure he jumped over the edge ten minutes before she left. Since the prom where Aarabelle was adamant they were just friends, she and Chase have grown very close. He's a good kid, though. He came to the house and asked Liam for permission to ask his daughter out.

Liam, of course, is a dick and made him sweat it out.

I bet he wishes he said no now.

But, seriously, Chase is a good kid.

"Where is your son?" I ask absently. It's been quiet the last hour in the garage where he was working on his bike.

"He's in the garage . . ."

"Go bother him. Maybe he needs some help while you wait."

Liam kisses my forehead and heads out the door.

I watch as he leaves, admiring the view of his ass. Sometimes, I can't help it. He's just too cute.

Instead of waiting in here, I walk out to the porch with my coffee cup and curl up on the wicker couch. I love sitting out here at night. I can hear the waves crashing against the shore. The salt air calms my soul, and it always makes me grateful I got to stay in this house.

"Are you fucking *crazy*?" I hear Liam's deep voice yell.

"Dad!"

"Don't you dare *Dad* me!"

"It isn't what it looks like!"

Oh, this can't be good. I place the cup down and jog around the front of the house to see what the yelling is about.

When I get to the garage door, I see Shane pulling his shirt on and a girl doing the same.

"Fucking hell, Shane!" I say with horror in my voice.

"I swear, we were—"

Liam slaps Shane in the back of the head. "Shut your mouth."

"But she—"

Another smack.

"I didn't give you permission to talk. I'm contemplating letting you breathe much longer," Liam says through gritted teeth.

"You should head home," I say to the girl, whose face is bright red as she refuses to look anywhere but at the ground.

Shane opens his mouth to say something and Liam steps closer, grabbing his neck. "Not a word."

Why is it the bigger they get the bigger my fears are? Can't we go back to diapers and duct tape? Anything other than condoms.

She scurries out just as headlights illuminate the driveway.

Great. Aarabelle is here now and is going to get the wrath of this fiasco.

"I'm sorry, I'm sorry," Aara says as she and Chase walk up the drive. "I swear, we weren't doing anything."

"No one! No. One. Other than me and your mother should be having sex in this house. No one. Do you understand?" Liam explodes, his eyes firmly locked on his son as Aara and Chase come to stand next to me. Clearly, my daughter doesn't think she is included in that edict, which tells me she isn't doing anything she shouldn't be.

Like an idiot, Shane laughs, which has both Aarabelle and I looking on in horror.

"What are you talking about?" she finally asks, drawing Liam's attention.

No. No. No. Aara. You should know better than to talk when Liam has that look on his face.

"Did you have sex? Is that why you were late?" Liam, still holding Shane's neck asks as he moves toward her.

"No! God! We were stuck in traffic!"

He turns to Chase. "I swear that if you were at some sleazy motel or steaming up the back seat, boy . . ."

Chase lifts his hands. "I swear, Mr. Dempsey, it was traffic."

"Liam." I step in.

"These kids are nuts, sweetheart! They're nuts! I catch one with his pants down and the other . . . well, I don't know what she did, but . . ."

Or maybe their father is the one who's nuts, but I decide to keep that one in. I think the hardest thing about parenting is the loss of control.

The older they get, the less control you have. It is just the way of life.

"Everything okay, Lee?" My elderly neighbor asks from the window.

"We're fine, Mrs. DeMatteo!"

I wave and really hope she doesn't have her hearing aids in.

"Sorry, Mrs. D," Liam yells.

"All right then, honey. I just heard the shouting." She blows him a kiss and then shuts the window.

I can't even with the women when it comes to him. He's like catnip to the opposite sex. I know he's beyond good-looking, but come on. It isn't like he's God's gift to women. I live with him. I know this to be true.

"Now that you've announced to our neighbors that we're the only ones allowed to have sex, would you like to take this inside?"

Liam releases a heavy sigh through his nose. "You"—he points to Chase—"you were to have her home on time. Did you do anything that I would want to kill you for? And don't lie because I'll know?"

"No, sir."

"You"—Liam points to Aarabelle—"get inside."

"Can I say good night to Chase?" she asks.

"Do you want me to show Chase where all his pressure points are located?"

"Good night, Aara!" Chase says as he climbs back in his car.

"See! He's smart." Liam looks at me. "Why did we get the dumb one?"

Oh, the come backs I have for this. "Because he's half yours . . ."

He grabs Shane by the back of the neck and marches forward. "Well, I'm about to slap the stupid out of him."

I don't know who he's trying to fool, he would never raise a hand to either of them, but Shane's eyes widen.

Our children have grown up with the knowledge that most of the men in their lives are trained in some pretty scary things. Liam's way to bond with Shane was to teach him a lot of them as well. They love to rough house, roll around, and see how many dead legs they can give each other before someone cries.

Sometimes I wonder if maybe he ate lead paint or something.

"Shane, go up to your room. Your dad and I will be up in bit to talk about this. Once we've calmed down enough not to hang you on the flagpole by your underwear."

"I'm sorry, Mom."

I close my eyes and nod. "Just go to your room and leave your phone on the counter on your way up."

He walks inside the house, and Liam wraps his arms around my waist.

"Tell me they weren't . . ." I beg.

"They weren't. I don't know if they planned to."

"Great."

"I know, they were on top of Robin," he grumbles.

His car. He's worried about his freaking car. "God forbid."

"What if they scratched her?"

Liam and his car need a moment. He's had this freaking

thing since before we started dating. It's basically a museum in the garage. Every few days, he comes out here, talks to her—because the car is real to him—and tinkers with it.

"I'm sure Robin is just fine."

"If she isn't, he's going to pay."

I don't doubt that. "Don't you think you should be more concerned that he had a girl here and was missing clothing?"

"No." He scoffs. "I love that car."

"And you don't love your kids?"

"Not as much as Robin. I've had her longer, she's good to me, and doesn't give me half the headaches those two do."

We walk over to the porch and sit together. His arms wrap around me from behind while my head rests on his chest.

"Well, I'm not worried about her."

"Honestly, I'm concerned about everything. They're growing up so fast, and it feels like we're losing control."

I nod because I had been thinking the same thing moments ago. "They just think they know it all."

"How wrong they are . . ."

"No shit. We didn't learn how wrong we were until we were in our thirties."

Liam laughs lightly. "And even then, we're still figuring out we were dumb as fuck."

"This parenting gig sucks." I sigh.

"There's no one else I'd rather suck with, though."

I smile and look back at him. "Same here."

"Good thing you're really good at sucking." He laughs at his dirty joke.

"You know . . ." I sit up to get a better look at him. "You're able to turn anything back to sex. No wonder our son was in there on top of your car and doing whatever he was doing."

He shrugs. "He's a Dempsey. We're natural ladies men."

"Oh, for the love of . . ."

"You can trademark that line, baby."

"Sometimes I wonder what the hell I was thinking when I fell in love with you." It's a lie.

I know exactly what I was thinking—*here's a man who loves me in my most broken state. He's kind, loyal, protective, and wants to do the right thing, even if he has to walk away to save us all.*

Liam walked beside me during the most difficult part of my life. He was self-sacrificing at every turn.

My life could've gone a very different way if it weren't for him.

My heart might still be broken, but his unyielding love healed every last broken shard.

"You were thinking that I had the biggest—"

"Heart."

"Wrong body part, Lee."

I shrug. "This is why our son thinks the way he does . . . you."

"Please, like your eyes didn't go to my dick when I said that." He laughs.

"Whatever," I say as he pulls me back against his chest and I tilt my head so I can look up at him.

"I love you, Lee."

"I'm glad you do."

"Yeah?"

"Most of the time," I joke.

"Good."

I stare into Liam's blue eyes and smile. "I love you too, you know?"

"I do, but you gave me a defective child that we must return."

Ugh. The boy. The boy with raging hormones and the charm of his father.

"Listen, that kid is all you, so . . . good luck with him. I'm way too young to be a grandmother, so you need to scare the hell out of him or something."

"You'd be the prettiest grandma around."

He is *not* funny. "I'll handle Aarabelle being late. You handle Shane being an idiot."

He nods. "Fine, but let her know I'll be watching and remind her that I know how to hide a body."

Sad part is that he's not kidding. He really does know how to.

"And after that, we'll have some wine," I say, pushing myself to my feet.

"Deal, but you have to promise to be naked tonight."

I lean down, pressing a quick kiss to his lips. "Maybe, considering we are the only ones who are allowed to have sex in this house."

He kisses me this time. "Damn right, I'm about to cockblock these kids until they're thirty."

My head falls back as I laugh.

Only Liam can take the crazy and make it feel like it's going to be okay.

If you enjoyed Cockblocked, be sure to grab Consolation, and find out how Natalie and Liam found each other. Or you can grab Beloved (Book 1 in the Salvation Series) FREE for a limited time!

To read an EXCLUSIVE preview of my upcoming novel, sign up for my newsletter and you'll get a look at it before anyone else!

CHRISTMAS SCENE

CHAPTER ONE

"Sweetheart? Could you come in here?" Liam calls from the living room where he's supposed to be putting up the tree. This can't be good.

"What the hell?" I gasp as I walk into the room. Only him. Only my husband would have the tree roped to the ceiling and tied to the leg of the couch and the piano. "Liam! It's not a tent! It's a tree."

"It kept falling, so I fixed it," he beams with pride.

I don't even have words to explain the idiocy that resides in this otherwise gorgeous, talented, and actual genius of a man. I mean, really? He tied the tree up?

"Fix it again! How can you think this works? Aarabelle is going to trip over the ropes, not to mention your son who puts everything in his mouth!" I shake my head in disbelief.

He crosses his arms and looks over his handiwork. "It'll be fine. It's upright, which it wasn't fifteen minutes ago. Plus, I didn't even have to use tape."

My life with Liam is always full of surprises. He keeps me on my toes, that's for sure. It's Shane's first Christmas and we've gone all out. We were in Arkansas visiting my parents, then we flew up to Ohio to see his dad. Luckily, we were able to get home to have Christmas under our own roof. But that meant that we got the last tree on the lot. It was two feet too tall for our ceiling, and they cut it down, but it's still too big.

This is just ludicrous. "You can't be serious, Liam! No. There's rope practically nailed to the ceiling!"

I start to walk out of the room before I say something stupid —holiday cheer and all that—but his strong arms wrap around my torso. As much as I want to fight it, I can't. His touch causes my heart to swell, and my anger to ebb. Everything about our time together is special.

"Lee," he murmurs in my ear. "There's a chance I won't be here next Christmas. Do you really want to spend this one pissed about a tree?"

Damn him.

My head lolls to the side as his scruff rubs against my neck. "Why do you make it so easy to forgive you?"

"Because you love me."

"And yet you piss me off constantly."

"Athair!" Aarabelle runs in the room, greeting Liam with the Gaelic for "father" and stops, looking up at the tree. "Uh oh," she says as she turns to Liam.

We both laugh and he kisses my neck. "Go make us a plate for Santa, woman." He slaps my ass, gently pushing me towards the door.

I turn and glare at him. "You're lucky you're so hot."

I head into the kitchen and arrange the plate of protein bars— apparently Santa needs to refuel at our house, and no one was letting me bake...they've been to that shitshow—then grab a beer. These were Liam's demands—Santa needs a "man snack" because "That cookies and milk bullshit ain't gonna keep him going. He's got shit to do." So, we'll apparently teach our children that Santa likes health bars and booze at our stop.

"Lee!" Liam yells. "Get your butt out here!"

Our house looks like a bomb went off. Things are strewn

around every room, bags clog the hallway, it's a death trap. I grab the plate and Sam Adams and head into the living room.

I almost drop the plate.

I'm actually shocked that I don't drop the plate.

The tree is still hog tied. However, he now has Aarabelle tangled up in the lights, and Shane is banging together two ornaments that have miraculously not yet shattered. Liam is on a ladder with the net lights. "Did your parents ever put up a tree?" I ask as I head over to the kids. "How in the five minutes I was gone did you manage to make this worse?"

"Mommy!" Aarabelle turns around tying herself up further. "Pwetty lights!"

"Yes, baby." I start to untangle her, and take the glass ornaments away from Shane. Once I have them both safely away from their father and his mess that is our tree, I head over to try to help.

Liam throws the lights to the ground. "They won't go around the rope."

"You mean the rope nailed to the ceiling?" I roll my eyes. "How did you make it through BUDs? Don't you guys have to build things and survive with a pack of matches and a stick?"

Liam throws a twig at me. "I'm not MacGyver. Or Chuck Norris?"

"No," I smirk. "He would have had the tree up, level, and had a fire started in the fireplace at Shane's age. He could've made the tree put itself up while he grilled a side of cow and downed a bottle of whiskey. Chuck Norris is a bad ass."

"So you have a thing for Chuck Norris?"

"I have a thing for men who can *fix* things. Unlike my jackass husband who requires rope or duct tape."

Liam climbs down from the ladder with a gleam in his eyes. His envelopes me as he pulls me close. "I fixed you."

"I didn't know I was broken," I smile.

But he did fix me. He fixed all of us. His love, patience, and persistence are what kept me whole. Liam filled the gaps I didn't know were there. Now, he's the glue that holds us all together.

"Not broken, just cracked. Maybe dented a little too." He leans down and presses his lips to mine before I can retort.

"I'll give you dented."

"You could just give me a kiss," he suggests.

I lean back and let out a heavy breath to toy with him. Liam squeezes me tight and rubs his scruffy chin on my throat. "Liam!" I protest.

"Kiss me," he demands.

My hands grip his face as I crush my lips to his. He holds me close as his hands glide up my back keeping me against him. The tree tied to the ceiling, the kids wrapped in lights, the mess, and the crazy all fade away. While the kiss is brief, it's passion mixed with adoration. I lose myself in Liam until someone pulls on my leg.

"Mommy!"

We break apart with a laugh.

"Mommy! Santa coming?"

I crouch down, tap the tip of her nose, and smile. "Yes, princess. Let's get ready for bed so Santa can come."

"I miss the days when she didn't have some kind of radar for whenever I touch you."

I laugh. "She just hates when you're not paying attention to her."

"Is that so, Aara?" He swoops her into his arms. "Is that it? You want my attention?" he says playfully. She giggles as he tosses her in the air and catches her. I grab Shane as the sounds of her giggles fill the air.

Once we get the kids to bed, Liam starts to bring down all the gifts from the attic. Oh, the joys that are coming when he has to put together Aarabelle's dollhouse. I'm half excited, half terrified.

"Did you buy the entire toy store?"

"When they're little it just seems like a lot. Stop bitching.

Think of this as a workout. Which by the way, your abs are looking a little less … firm?"

"Funny." His eyes narrow at my jab. Of course, this is the furthest thing from the truth. Liam works out every day, even if he can't get to the gym. It was a sight to see him doing push-ups with Aarabelle on his back. A damn sexy sight.

"I thought so." I shrug, giving him my best innocent smirk.

He stalks forward. "Let's not forget what happened the last time you insinuated I was fat."

My mind flashes back to that night. The night when things shifted in our friendship. The night I really saw him differently. I shake my head, "Not this time, Dreamboat. You've got work to do."

His face falls. "Work?"

"Who do you think is going to put together that dollhouse?"

"You're fucking kidding me."

"Nope. Get busy."

He grabs the beer off the table, shoves the excess rope and lights to the side while I attempt to decorate the tree. The next few hours pass as I curse Liam and he curses the toy companies.

Liam throws the screwdriver and the directions over his head. "I swear to God! The people who make these things are evil. They know fathers around the world are up all night trying to figure out where piece J34 is because it's a screw that looks like all the other damn screws!"

"You use any kind of 'fixing' apparatus on that dollhouse and you'll never get laid again," I warn.

"You can't resist me."

"Try me."

He grabs the paper and gets back to work. After another two hours and countless beers, the dollhouse and Shane's play gym are put together—correctly, with only a small pile of leftover mystery parts that he conveniently drops in the trash as I put on the bows. We head upstairs, hoping for just a few hours of sleep.

I head to the bathroom to get ready, and stop to stare in the mirror. I swear I didn't have these crow's feet yesterday.

In the mirror I see Liam leaning against the door. "You look beautiful."

"You lie."

"You're perfect, Lee." He stands behind me and pulls me against his chest. "You have no idea how much I love you, sweetheart."

I lean back, resting my head against his shoulder. "I have a pretty good idea, but it doesn't come close to how much I love you."

"Doubtful."

We stay like this, letting the moment linger as long as possible. Between our jobs, his absences, two kids, a house, and just life … they're few and far between.

"Now," Liam's husky voice echoes in the room. "I want to open my present."

His lips find purchase right below my ear. "Do you now? Have you been nice?"

"Very," he kisses me again.

"Maybe you're on the naughty list."

Liam's tongue glides down my neck as he slips off the strap to my camisole. "Only with you."

His hands move up my stomach as he cups my breasts. I let out a moan, tilting my head back as he massages and pulls. He grips my hips and spins me. Without a heartbeat passing, his lips find mine. Our tongues slide against each other's as he holds the back of my head and my ass. We kiss as if we haven't had each other in months. Our breathing is heavy as he breaks away from me. His eyes lock on mine and he doesn't have to say anything. I know what he needs—me.

Liam leaves soon, and it's been weighing heavy on both of us. Another deployment. Another sacrifice of our time from each other, but this is our life, and I knew it was coming.

"I love you. So much." I let him know the only thing in my heart right now.

"I know. And I love you. Now, shut up so I can show you just how much."

I press my lips together and Liam lifts my top off. Lucky for me, he's just wearing his boxers so I have easy access. I roam my hands over every inch of his chest. I marvel in the ridges and planes of his body. God, I'm a lucky woman.

He hoists me up and places me on the sink. The cold granite causes me to gasp. Liam drops to his knees, pulls my panties off, and throws my legs over his shoulders. My head falls back, hitting the mirror as he swipes his tongue against my clit.

I moan as he continues to drive me to the edge. My hands grip the counter while Liam devours me. He moves in a rhythm that's both maddening and intoxicating. "Liam," I beg. "Please, I need you."

He bites down and I fall apart. I cry out his name as he relentlessly circles and sucks. He stops, removes his boxers, then pulls me to the edge. "Merry Christmas, sweetheart," he says before entering me slowly.

"Best. Present. Ever."

After we finish making love, Liam helps me to bed. His arms open wide and I tuck myself into the crook of his shoulder. While cuddling isn't his favorite thing, he knows how much it means to me. So many nights I'll spend cold and alone in this bed, so when he's home, I need his warmth.

"Goodnight, Lee."

"Goodnight, babe."

We drift off, wrapped up in each other.

"Mommy! Athair! Mommy! Santa tame!" I swear I literally just closed my eyes.

Liam lifts Aara into our bed and pulls her to his chest. "He did?"

"Come see! Come see, Athair! Santa tame!" She squeals as he tickles her.

"Well, let's go see!" Liam is more excited than anyone. Then again, after putting together a dollhouse for four hours, I can imagine he wants to see the look on her face.

Aarabelle hops down from the bed and runs into Shane's room. "Wate up, Shane! Santa tame!" She pokes his side through the rails.

I lift him up, and we follow Aarabelle downstairs, her lovely curls fluttering out behind her as she flies.

A knock on the door halts us both. Even still my heart stops a little. That sound takes me back, no matter how hard I try to stop it. I know it's crazy. I know that Liam is safe right now, but being notified your husband is dead, is something I'll never forget.

"Expecting someone?" he asks.

"No, are you?"

We haven't seen anyone while we we did the tour-the-country thing. So I have no idea who could be here at six o'clock in the morning.

Aarabelle rushes to the door, abandoning the presents. Liam scoops her up as I go to get Shane's bottle. He doesn't care about anything but his food. My eyes practically bug out of my head when I enter the living room. They're all here.

Every last one of them.

Jackson, Catherine, Mark, Aaron, and Quinn. At six o'clock in the morning, they're all here.

"Mommy!" Aarabelle screams as her "uncles" pass her around. "Santa tame to everybody's house!"

"Merry Christmas! I've come to bestow my divine wisdom on this Holy holiday. Give ol' Father Mark a hug, huh?" Mark heads toward me with his arms wide.

"You're an idiot. Now when does that ordination expire again?"

"You love me," he retorts.

He takes a second to take in the scene and starts laughing hysterically. "Dude, you're a little special you know that? But nice work with the rope."

I groan. "Do. Not. Encourage. Him. What are you doing here?"

"We missed you, Sparkles."

"No, seriously, why are you all here?"

Catherine puts her arms out for the baby. "Because we're family and we wanted to spend Christmas morning with our family."

Jackson encircles his arm around her waist as she holds Shane. "Liam arranged it. He knew you'd want this Christmas to be special."

I look over at my husband who is on the floor with Aarabelle. She runs between Mark and Liam, basking in the attention over-load. Aaron and Quinn sit on the couch laughing and shoving each other. Catherine and Jackson are in their own little bubble as they gaze at Shane and the dreams for their future. Liam continues to give me things I never knew I needed. He planned this morning for me. Surrounded by the people I love. Sure, they're a little crazy, but that's what makes it so perfect. He knew this would be the only gift that mattered, and once again—he gave it to me.

Liam catches my eyes and winks. I head over to him and he pulls me close. "Happy?"

I gaze into his blue eyes, "I'm happy with you."

"Good," he kisses my nose. "Merry Christmas, sweetheart. This is only the beginning."

LOST LOVE LETTERS

LIAM LETTER

S weetheart,

IT's BEEN two years since we first got together. Times where I'm sure you've wanted to slap me, but ultimately you see my charm. I've always wanted a marriage like my parents. It was something I thought was untouchable and rare. While we don't share what they had, we have something much better.

You make me the man that I am. Everyday I strive to be more for you. I want to be the kind of man that you're proud of. I want for Aarabelle to look at the way I treat you, and find someone to love her that way or better. I might fail at times, but never doubt my love for you. Ever.

Our relationship is never easy, but then I think that most things worth a damn aren't. We should have to work for this, because you're worth that and more. When I piss you off, when I make you wish I was on deployment, or when you think I'm not giving enough—punch me in the throat. I'll deserve it because you don't deserve anything less than the best of me.

Now that I've said all that mushy shit, how about you get naked and let me show you how much I love you. I've got your eggroll this time.

Love,
     Liam

DIAPER SCENE - ALTERNATE POV

Lee heads up the stairs coughing and dragging ass. I hate that she's so sick. I look down in my arms, and realize I now have care of a child.

Well, I'm fucked.

I debate calling my mom to ask what exactly I should do. She would probably laugh at me then hang up. There was no way I couldn't help her though. Natalie looked like death. Plus, this should score me some serious brownie points.

Kids like television…I think. I decide that should be our first thing. Aarabelle and I sit on the couch as I turn on the Packers game.

"Alright, Aara. Let's see if Rodgers is going to screw it up or we're going to kick some ass," she laughs. "Shit. I probably shouldn't say ass. Or shit. Fuck, I'll shut up."

Now I'm talking to a baby. And cursing at her too. There go those brownie points.

We spend the next hour or so taking every possible toy in the house out. She plays with this weird ball thing that spits them out the top. Whoever thought flying balls was a good idea should be shot.

Aara starts to really fuss as panic begins to rise. "What do you need? Food? Toys? Want to go outside?"

I pick her up, and the smell hits me straight in the face.

"What the hell does she feed you?" I ask aloud. I've been around guys after field meals that don't smell as bad as this.

"Okay, diaper." I say looking around the room. "Where are they?" I ask hoping she can at least point. Instead, she just cries louder.

My phone rings and I pray it's someone who knows something about kids. I look down only to see Quinn's number.

"Yo," I answer while searching for the stash.

"Are you at Lee's?"

He's a real Einstein. "Yeah, she's sick so I'm watching Aarabelle. What gave it away? The screaming baby in the background?"

Quinn laughs so loud I have to move the phone away. "Dude. She must be on her death bed to let that happen."

"Fu—dge you. I've got this. She's a baby not a bomb."

"Right," he laughs again. "Well, while you're playing house I'm heading to get laid."

I hate him. I really hope his dick falls off. "Good for you."

"Hell yeah it is."

"Do you know how to change a diaper?" I ask absently. Quinn has a younger brother so maybe there's a chance.

"Yeah, do you?"

"You're so damn helpful. Look," I glance at Aarabelle lying in her crap on the floor. "She's rancid. I need help."

"Well, Dreamboat...good luck." He hangs up. I swear I'm going to punch him in the balls next time I see him.

I see the bag that Lee carries around and start to rummage through. Ha! Diapers.

"Okay, Aarabelle. We got this."

She just stares at me. Yeah, I'm pretty sure this is going to be a mess.

I unsnap her shirt thing, waiting for some kind of divine

intervention. Okay, this should be easy. I can take apart an M-16 with my eyes closed, jump out of a plane undetected—I got this.

"Maybe there's a Youtube video?" Aara just stares at me. "Yeah, I know I'm an idiot, but whatever." I grab the diaper, and lay it flat. Once I pull down the dirty diaper, I immediately regret it. "How in the world did you do that?"

I contemplate going to wake Lee, but then I'll have to listen to how I couldn't handle it. Defeat is not in my vocabulary.

I get her cleaned up without any catastrophe and then prepare for phase two.

The diaper is in place, but when I pull the tab, it rips off. What the hell? I try the other side and that one does the same thing.

I grab the spare diaper and try it more gently but this one the entire stretchy side comes off. "What the?"

Aara starts to cry. "It's okay…shhh." I try to calm her, but she cries louder.

I look around for something to close this thing since I have no idea where the rest of her diapers are. "Don't move." I say standing with my hands out hoping she'll stay put.

There's no tape anywhere, but I remember in my bag I have rope. I'll just tie it on. I rush back over where she's still crying, and I start to talk to her. Aarabelle doesn't relax as her legs go flying all over the place. By some miracle, I manage to get one diaper on the front and one covering the back. That should do it. The tab on the one side sticks so I try to arrange the rope holding the other.

"See, I told you," I smile holding her up. The diaper stays put, for now.

I grab the bottle that's in the fridge, and rush back in the room. Seriously, it's worse than an explosion. I shut the lights off so I don't have to look at it. Once I get Aara on the couch she drinks her bottle as we both relax.

Crisis averted.

KEEP UP WITH CORINNE

If you'd like to just keep up with my sales and new releases, you can follow me on BookBub or sign up for text alerts!
BookBub: https://www.bookbub.com/authors/corinne-michaels

Text Alerts: Text cmbooks to 77948

If you're on Facebook, join my private reader group for special updates and a lot of fun.
Corinne Michaels Books Facebook Group
➙http://on.fb.me/1tDZ8Sb

Made in the USA
Columbia, SC
19 October 2018